Dear mouse friends,
Welcome to the world of

Geronimo Stilton

THE RODENT'S GAZETTE
EDITORIAL STAFF

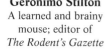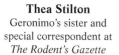

Geronimo Stilton
A learned and brainy
mouse; editor of
The Rodent's Gazette

Thea Stilton
Geronimo's sister and
special correspondent at
The Rodent's Gazette

Trap Stilton
An awful joker;
Geronimo's cousin and
owner of the store
Cheap Junk for Less

Benjamin Stilton
A sweet and loving
nine-year-old mouse;
Geronimo's favorite
nephew

Geronimo Stilton

HUG A TREE, GERONIMO

Scholastic Inc.

Published by Scholastic Inc., *Publishers since 1920*, 557 Broadway, New York, NY 10012. SCHOLASTIC and associated logos are trademarks and/or registered trademarks of Scholastic Inc.

Stilton is the name of a famous English cheese. It is a registered trademark of the Stilton Cheese Makers' Association. For more information, go to www.stiltoncheese.com.

This book is a work of fiction. Names, characters, places, and incidents are either the product of the author's imagination or are used fictitiously, and any resemblance to actual persons, living or dead, business establishments, events, or locales is entirely coincidental.

ISBN 978-1-338-21524-3

Text by Geronimo Stilton
Original title *La leggenda della grande quercia*
Cover by Danilo Barozzi
Illustrations by Silvia Bigolin and Daria Cerchi
Graphics by Michela Battaglin and Marta Lorini

Special thanks to AnnMarie Anderson
Translated by Anna Pizzelli
Interior design by Maria Mercado

10 9 8 7 6 5 4 3 2 1   18 19 20 21 22

Printed in the U.S.A.   40

First printing 2018

THIS IS HOW IT ALL BEGAN . . .

The story you are about to read is an *incredible* tale of nature, love, and friendship. But wait! First let me introduce myself: **MY** name is Stilton, *Geronimo Stilton*, and I am the publisher of **The Rodent's Gazette**, the most famouse newspaper on Mouse Island!

This is the story of an **adventure** that changed my life **forever** . . .

What an adventure!

It was the first day of spring, and I was riding my bike to work . . .

As I pedaled through the streets of New Mouse City, I looked up at the beautiful blue sky peeking between the tall buildings, and I began to **daydream**. Oh, how I wished I could head straight to the **park**! There, I would lie in the grass, looking at the **clouds**. I would listen to the birds **CHIRPING**, and I would smell the sweet spring flowers as I thought of ideas for my next novel . . .

Ring! Ring!

My cell phone interrupted my reverie. I answered the call.

"Grandson!" shouted my grandfather. "I know you're thinking of skipping

Grandson!

Grandfather William Shortpaws

WORK today! I know you very well: **every** year when spring comes, your snout is **UP**, looking at the clouds, and you neglect your work at the paper! But I know how to get you **back on track**!"

"B-but, Grandfather, I'm riding my bike to work at *The Rodent's Gazette* right now!" I argued.

"Aha, see?!" **Grandfather** barked back. "I was right! You're tooling around town on your bicycle instead of buckling down at the office to **WORK**, **WORK**, **WORK**! This is what happens to you every **SPRING**! Come on, Grandson!

"Get to the office right away! Chop, chop! I want you here in **ten seconds**!"

"Ten seconds?!" I protested. "But that's imposs —"

He started counting down: "**Ten . . . nine . . . eight . . .**"

MOLDY MOZZARELLA! All I could do was pedal as quickly as possible. My grandfather could be so annoying!

I arrived at the entrance to *The Rodent's Gazette*, panting. My tongue was hanging out.

"**Three** . . . **two** . . . **one** . . . **zero**!" Grandfather exclaimed. "Ah, there you are! From now on, no more **slacking off**! Thanks to this **slacker alarm**, I can keep track of everyone, especially you, Grandson!"

I groaned. Not the **slacker alarm**!

THE SLACKER ALARM

The slacker alarm is a very complicated tool that Grandfather William invented to keep track of slackers at *The Rodent's Gazette* (especially his grandson, Geronimo Stilton!).

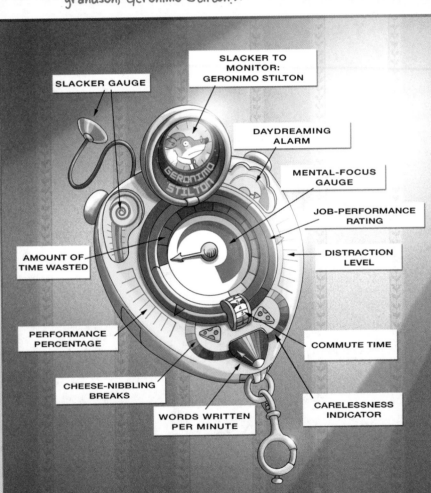

SLACKER TO MONITOR: GERONIMO STILTON

SLACKER GAUGE

DAYDREAMING ALARM

MENTAL-FOCUS GAUGE

JOB-PERFORMANCE RATING

DISTRACTION LEVEL

AMOUNT OF TIME WASTED

COMMUTE TIME

PERFORMANCE PERCENTAGE

CHEESE-NIBBLING BREAKS

WORDS WRITTEN PER MINUTE

CARELESSNESS INDICATOR

"What a *mouserific* tool!" my grandfather muttered under his breath, smiling to himself. "Now let's talk about you, Geronimo. I know you haven't started **writing** your new book yet."

"B-but, Grandfather," I squeaked, "I can't write **on command**. I need inspiration! I need a fabumouse idea! I can't just write **meaningless words**."

"Stop making excuses!" my grandfather grumbled. "Sit down and start writing instead of daydreaming. And remember: that **slacker alarm** is monitoring you!"

Oh, how annoying!

Argh!

A BAD CASE OF WRITER'S BLOCK

I sat at my desk for **hours** and **hours**, trying to write my book. I tugged at my whiskers in **frustration**, but at the end of the day, the page was still **blank**. I had the worst case of writer's block!

Oh, how annoying!

Argh!

All of a sudden, a purple whirlwind **blew** into my office. It was my friend CREEPELLA VON CACKLEFUR!

She leaned on my desk and blew a thousand kisses at me. You should know that Creepella likes to tell everymouse she's my girlfriend, but we're just friends!

"DARLING, today is the first day of spring," she squeaked. "What are you doing sitting in your office like a moldy mummy? Let's go for a walk in the park!"

Right then, my friend **Hercule Poirat** popped into my office.

"Gerrykins, I really need your **help**!" he squeaked. "You see, I'm trying to solve a really **puzzling** mystery . . ."

I could hear the **slacker alarm** buzzing from the hallway (my grandfather must have been **LINGERING** there!).

"**Bzzzz!** Geronimo Stilton has not started working yet," a mechanical voice said. "**Bzzzz!** He has not written a single word. **Bzzzz!** What a slacker!"

I shook my snout in frustration.

"**MOLDY MOZZARELLA**!" I exclaimed. "**Grandfather** wants me to work, **CREEPELLA** wants me to go for a walk in the park, and Hercule wants me to solve a mystery! All I want to do is **write my novel**!"

At that moment, my sister, Thea, and her friend *Flora van der Plant* burst into the office. Flora is an **herbalist** and an expert on medicinal plants and essential oils. She has her own natural beauty product and herbal tea company. Flora, Thea, and Creepella are **good friends**.

"What's wrong, Geronimo?" my sister asked right away.

"Yes, you look **terrible**!" Flora added sympathetically.

"Nothing!" I replied, exasperated. "I'm just trying to write! But

These three mice are a special group of friends who are also journalists! Thea Stilton is a correspondent for *The Rodent's Gazette*. She travels the world seeking adventures and the latest fabumouse stories. Creepella von Cacklefur writes for *The Shivery News* in Mysterious Valley. And Flora van der Plant writes "Dear Flora," an herbalist advice column that appears in *The Rodent's Gazette*. She talks (and writes) about plants as if they're her friends!

Grandfather is keeping **track** of me with the **slacker alarm**, Hercule needs help solving a *mystery*, and Creepella is trying to get me to take a break and go walk in the **park**!"

"Poor Gerryberry!" Thea teased.

But Flora rushed to my defense.

"You do look *tense*," she said. "That won't help with your writing! You could use a **calming** cup of herbal tea. I'll make you a special, stress-reducer blend!"

A moment later, she, Thea, and Creepella rolled a *gigantic* tea cart into my office.

Flora immediately whipped up an enormouse, **hot**, *steaming* mug of tea in a cheese-print mug.

"Drink it!" the three mice commanded in unison.

Herbal tea is made from the seeds, leaves, roots, or bark of plants. Soaking these in hot water releases vitamins and minerals, creating a drink that's tasty and good for you, too!

IT WASN'T ME . . . IT WAS MY COUSIN!

When I finished drinking the herbal tea, I **burped** so loudly everything in my office **shook**.

Suddenly, I realized I was **hungry**!

I opened the drawer to my desk looking

I drank the tea down in one gulp!

Then I let out a huge burp!

for a yummy cheese-filled chocolate. I love them so much I always have a box stashed there, along with some candy, cookies, and other delicious snacks.

I pulled out the box and opened it to discover . . .

Squeak!

THE BOX WAS EMPTY!

I decided to munch on a chocolate . . .

. . . but the box was empty!

"Where are my chocolates?" I wailed.

I was positive my cousin TRAP had eaten them. He has the bad habit of going through my things and devouring any snacks he finds.

Oh, how annoying!

A second later, I heard a strange roar. All of a sudden, a mouse on a motorcycle burst into my office!

Caught you, Stilton!

Er...

It was my super-healthy, super-fit, super-muscular, and super-energetic friend Dr. Otto Cheesecake. He's the official dietician for the staff of **The Rodent's Gazette**, and he talks about healthy eating habits an awful lot for a mouse named *Cheesecake*!

"Ah, Stilton, admit it!" he squeaked. "I caught you with chocolate in your paws!"

I gulped, feeling embarrassed.

"It's not my *fault*, Doctor!"

"Tell me the truth, Stilton," he prodded me, chuckling. "How many cheesy chocolates did you eat?

Dr. Otto Cheesecake

He is one of Thea's friends and, like her, he loves motorcycles. He is Geronimo's personal dietician, and he writes "You Are What You Eat," a column in *The Rodent's Gazette*. He believes wholesome foods and exercise are the keys to good health. Dr. Cheesecake's slogan is: "Don't be a Cheesecake . . . Leave that to me!"

"You promised me you were going to take care of yourself and eat well!"

"B-but I didn't eat a single **one**!" I exclaimed. "It was my cousin Trap!"

He burst out laughing. Then he WINKED at me.

"Right," he said. "Blame your cousin! You know, this isn't the first time I've heard an excuse like that. My patients can be very creative. And what are you doing here in the office anyway? You're supposed to be at the gym right now exercising! Now let's see you do twenty-five jumping jacks . . . Let's go!"

"B-but, Doctor, I can't right now," I squeaked. "My grandfather, I mean, Creepella, I mean, Hercule . . . You see, the slacker alarm —"

 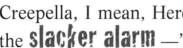

But he pushed me out the door.

"No more excuses, Stilton," he said. "Now go take a nice bike ride in the country. The fresh air will be good for you! You'll thank me for it later, or my name isn't **Dr. Cheesecake**!"

Go pedal, pedal, pedal!

BEST REGARDS AND CHEESE FOR ALL!

I decided to take Dr. Cheesecake's **ADVICE**. It had been impawssible to concentrate in the office anyway!

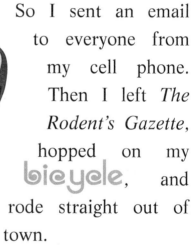

I'm taking some time off in search of inspiration. Best regards and cheese for all, Geronimo Stilton

So I sent an email to everyone from my cell phone. Then I left *The Rodent's Gazette*, hopped on my bicycle, and rode straight out of town.

I PEDALED and PEDALED and PEDALED . . .

and pedaled and pedaled and pedaled and p
and pedaled and pedaled and pedaled and pe
and pedaled and pedaled and pedaled and pedale
and pedaled and pedaled and pedaled and pedale
d pedaled and pedaled and pedaled and pedaled a
d pedaled and pedaled and pedaled and pedaled ana
d pedaled and pedaled and pedaled and pee
d pedaled and pedaled and pedaled and pedale
d pedaled and pedaled and pedaled and pedaled an
d pedaled and pedaled and pedaled and pedaled an
d pedaled and pedaled and pedaled and pedaled pea
d pedaled and pedaled and pedaled and pedaled and pea
l pedaled and pedaled and pedaled and pedaled and pedaled and pedaled and pec
l pedaled and pedaled and pedaled and pedaled and pedaled and pedaled and pec
pedaled and pedaled and pedaled and pedaled and pedaled and pedaled ana
pedaled and pedaled and pedaled and pedaled and pedaled and pedaled and p
pedaled and pedaled and pedaled and pedaled and pedaled and pedaled and pedaled a
edaled and pedaled and pedaled and pedaled and pedaled and pedaled and pedaled and p
edaled and pedaled and pedaled and pedaled and pedaled and pedaled and pedaled and pedaled and p

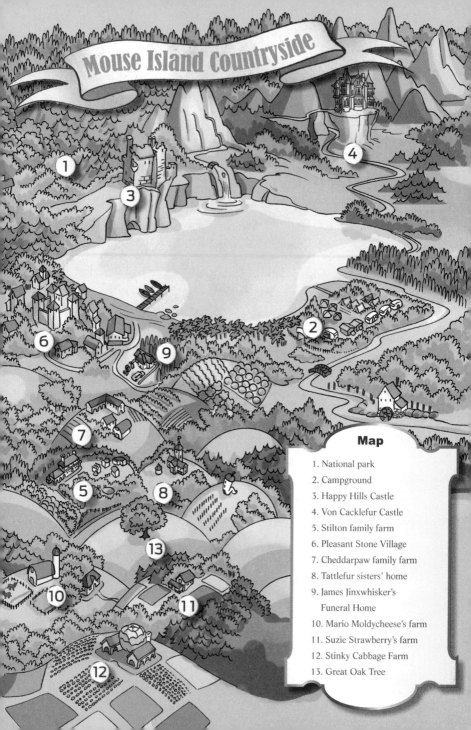

Mouse Island Countryside

Map

1. National park
2. Campground
3. Happy Hills Castle
4. Von Cacklefur Castle
5. Stilton family farm
6. Pleasant Stone Village
7. Cheddarpaw family farm
8. Tattlefur sisters' home
9. James Jinxwhisker's Funeral Home
10. Mario Moldycheese's farm
11. Suzie Strawberry's farm
12. Stinky Cabbage Farm
13. Great Oak Tree

. . . until I got to the countryside. Ah, how relaxing!

I was riding my bike up, up, up a narrow, hilly road leading through the woods.

The sun was warm on my fur, the birds were chirping, and a light breeze was blowing. Ah, the countryside is so charming!

A few minutes later, I had the feeling that I had been in that exact place before. HOW STRANGE!

I was deep in thought as I reached the top of the hill. And then I saw it — the most fabumouse view on Mouse Island! I was at the top of the famouse Happy Hills. Just looking at that beautiful landscape filled my heart with joy.

Then it hit me again — I felt like I had been in that exact place before. HOW STRANGE!

SNOUTDOWN IN A COMPOST HEAP!

I noticed a beautiful, tall, leafy OAK TREE on the hilltop right in front of me, and suddenly I knew why the place looked so familiar . . .

It wasn't a random oak tree, it was the LEGENDARY Great Oak!

When I was a mouselet, Grandfather William and my aunt Sweetfur used to take me to the Stilton family faRm in the Happy Hills for my summer vacation, and it had been right near that amazing tree!

Aunt Sweetfur had sold the farm years ago, but I wondered if it was STILL THERE. Excited at the thought of

seeing the place where I had made so many happy memories, I pedaled FASTER and FASTER.

I was flying down the hill, the wind in my fur, when I noticed a **TREE TRUNK** in the middle of the road.

SQUEAK!

I SLAMMED on the brakes, the bike screeched to a stop, and I flew

Help!

❷ I FLIPPED OVER THE HANDLEBARS . . .

Oops!

Yikes!

❶ I JAMMED ON THE BRAKES . . .

❸ I FLEW OVER THE TREE TRUNK . . .

over the trunk. I ended up snoutdown in a **puddle**. I continued to slide down the hill until I landed in a STINKY, SLIMY compost heap.

YUCK!

I stood up and tried to **clean off** my fur with some leaves. But the leaves just **stuck** to me!

4 I ENDED UP SNOUTDOWN IN A PUDDLE!

Ouch!

5 I SLID AND SLID AND SLID . . .

Ugh . . .

Yuck!

6 ALL THE WAY INTO A SMELLY COMPOST HEAP!

Oh, how do I always get myself into these **crazy messes**?

Suddenly, I heard *giggles* behind me.

"Tee, hee, hee!"

I turned to see three older rodents in **bright pink** dresses. They were laughing and pointing at me.

Tee, hee, hee!

Ha, ha!

It's really him: Geronimo Stilton!

The three Tattlefur sisters love to gossip. They write a column and a blog for the local paper called "True Tales of the Tattlefur Sisters." They know everything about everybody, and if there's nothing to find out, they make it up!

The first sister was peering at me through a pair of **binoculars**, the second was busy **taking notes**, and the third was already squeaking on the phone with a friend!

"**Guess what?**" she chattered. "Geronimo Stilton fell into a **compost heap**. I just saw it with my very own eyes! Yes, yes, I'm sure. It's really him: Geronimo Stilton, the publisher and editor in chief of **The Rodent's Gazette**. We'll be posting it later today on our blog, 'True Tales of the Tattlefur Sisters'!"

I was so *embarrassed* I turned as red as a tomato. Then I noticed a mysterious *leopard-patterned* limousine with tinted windows drive by.

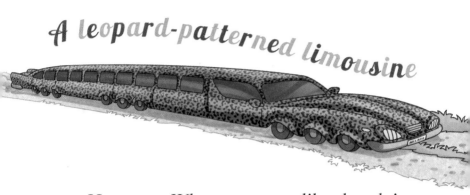

A leopard-patterned limousine

Hmm . . . What was a car like that doing out here in the **countryside**?

But before I could give the **strange** limousine much thought, I noticed a sign in front of me. I recognized the picture iMMEDiaTELy — it was the former Stilton family farm!

Squeak! So the farm where I used to go each summer when I was a mouseling was still right there. And more important, it was **for sale**!

YOU ARE A VERY LUCKY MOUSE!

As soon as I realized that the **farm** where I had spent so many happy summers was for sale, I knew it would be **fabumouse** to go back there with all my friends. I really wanted to **buy** it, but could I afford it?

I thought about it for a long time. Finally I called Aunt Sweetfur to ask her advice.

"My dear nephew," she squeaked, "follow your **heart** and you can't go wrong!"

So I hopped back on my bike and I pedaled and pedaled and pedaled all the way to Pleasant Stone Village. Once I arrived, I went straight to the office of **FIXER**

UPPER REALTY.

I told the owner that I had seen the sign and I wanted to buy the farm.

"What a coincidence!" he squeaked, a surprised look on his snout. "Someone else just called about the farm a moment ago. It was a **mysterious** rodent who didn't want to give me her name. She's on her way out here to the farm to buy it **as we squeak**!"

"Noooo!" I wailed. "I'm **too late**!"

He burst out laughing.

"Mr. Stilton, do you know you are a very **lucky** mouse?" he said, smiling. "You got

Congratulations!

What did I get myself into?

here first, so you're not too late. The farm is yours!"

With a shaky paw, I handed him a check.

"Congratulations," he said. "You are now the proud owner of a farmhouse and farm in the COUNTRYSIDE!"

Oh, what had I gotten myself into?

As I walked out the door, I saw the mysterious *leopard-patterned* limousine with tinted windows pull up. A female rodent wearing **DARK** sunglasses, a leopard-print dress, and **high-heeled** leopard-print shoes stepped out and hurried into the office. She was followed by three enormouse bodyguards.

Could that be the **mysterious** rodent interested in purchasing the farm? **Who knows?**

I didn't think about it for long because I was in a hurry to tell my friends and family the **EXCITING** news.

I **RODE** back to *The Rodent's Gazette* office as quickly as I could.

"My dear friends, I have *mouserific* news!" I squeaked as I opened the door. "I just discovered that the farm in the Happy Hills that I visited every summer when I was a

Hmm...

I taught you to ride your bicycle....

Thea learned to ride a horse....

Hercule solved his first case there....

I built a tree house for you...

mouseling is **still there**! And guess what? **I bought it!** You're all invited to come visit, once I make a few small **renovations** and repairs."

My friends surrounded and **hugged** me, squeaking happily.

Grandfather William shed a few tears and blew his nose in **my** tie.

"Well done, Grandson," he said proudly. "This was a great idea! I have so many happy memories of the farm. That's where I taught you to ride your **bicycle**, and it's where Thea learned to ride a horse.

Hercule solved his first case there, and I even **BUILT** you a tree house at the farm."

I sighed. "Won't it be **WONDERFUL** to be back there, Grandfather?" I asked.

"Yes, of course," he agreed. "But you know my **Motto**, right? **Work, Work, Work!** I expect only the best for the farm. I hope you have a plan for **fixing it up**, because I already have a plan for **tracking** your progress . . ."

So many memories!

Now get to work!

TINA SPICYTAIL
IS HERE!

I was almost knocked off my paws by a huge force. Was it a **CYCLONE**? A **tornado**?

No, it was my grandfather's cook and housekeeper, Tina Spicytail!

She has more energy than a baby hamster on a wheel, and she's strong enough to carry a tray of food **THREE TIMES HER SIZE**! She arrived, carrying a large silver tray loaded with food.

Tina Spicytail

"Here is your snack, Mr. William!" she announced.

Tina Spicytail
... and her seven nephews!

Tina Spicytail is Grandfather William's cook and housekeeper. She is an incredible chef known for her spectacular cheese lasagna and her delectable pies. She is the only one who can go snout-to-snout with Grandfather William. She always carries a silver rolling pin and a silver fork engraved with her initials.

These are her seven nephews:

MINO
the carpenter

RINO
the plumber

DINO
the gardener

LINO
the veterinarian

PINO
the mechanic

GINO
the beekeeper

TINO
the farmer

And this is Lina the hen, who is always pecking me!

"Yum!" he said as he rubbed his belly greedily. "Grandson, I have a great idea. I'll stay here at the office and you'll go to the farm with Tina. She'll keep track of your progress using the slacker alarm!"

If you know my grandfather at all, you know it's IMPOSSIBLE to argue with him (well, unless you're Tina!).

So I boarded my grandfather's cheese-colored camper along with my friends and family. My sister, Thea, got behind the wheel.

Three-cheese soufflé

Mini cheese snacks

Cheesy Jello-mold

Enormouse sandwich

Blueberry-pie

Eggplant-Parmesan

Pizza bites

During the drive to the farm, I started to **doubt** myself. Had I done the right thing? After all, I don't know **ANYTHING** about the country! How in the name of cheese was I going to fix up the farm and care for the Land and **animals**?

My whiskers trembled as I thought about all the work that had to be done. Suddenly, a friendly paw touched my shoulder.

Tina's tray

This large, silver, foldable tray is used to carry snacks for Grandfather William. It can hold up to thirty-three dishes, which he promptly gobbles up!

Mozzarella milkshake

Pineapple upside-down cake

Spectacular cheese lasagna

Spicytail special sundae

Strawberry cheesecake

"You look **nervous**, Geronimo," a voice squeaked. It was Flora van der Plant. "Don't worry; you aren't alone. We'll all work together!"

When we arrived at the farm, the sun was setting and the sky was turning a thousand different shades of pink. The countryside is so beautiful at sunset!

I stepped out of the camper to remove the **FOR SALE** sign in front of the farm and was greeted by a bunch of bright flashes. Holey cheese, it was the three Tattlefur sisters!

Grandfather's
Cheese-Colored Camper

This supercamper is longer than fifty mice standing tail-to-tail and is painted a deep cheddar yellow. It contains a kitchen, dining room, multiple bedrooms, and a library filled with books!

One of them waved a phone in front of my snout. **Squeak!** It showed a picture of me covered in leaves and **COMPOST** from the tips of my ears to the end of my tail!

Oh, how embarrassing!

My cousin Trap began to laugh and laugh.

"Cousin, you look so *silly* covered in compost and mud and leaves!" he tittered. "Ha, ha, ha! You'd better WATCH OUT for those Tattlefur sisters . . . They really got you!

Ha, ha, ha!"

Psst . . .

Psst . . .

Psst . . .

THE THREE TATTLEFUR SISTERS

HUGO THE ROOSTER

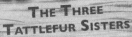

Try one!

SUZIE BLUEBERRY
She grows the biggest blueberries in the valley.

CAVALIER CABBAGE
He grows the stinkiest cabbage in the valley.

I'm going to get you!

RITA

THE CHEDDARPAW FAMILY
The happiest family in the valley

A Few Months Later . . .

We started renovating the farm right away and worked all **spring**, **summer**, and **fall**.

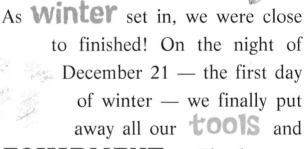

As **winter** set in, we were close to finished! On the night of December 21 — the first day of winter — we finally put away all our **tools** and **EQUIPMENT**. Thanks to everyone's help, we had done it! The **farm** was even nicer than it had been in the past. And I was starting to understand more and more about life in the country . . .

Spring

Summer

Fall

Winter

The Stilton Farm

OLIVE GROVE

ARCHERY RANGE

FARMHOUSE

WELL

SOCCER FIELD

GAZEBO

ENTRANCE

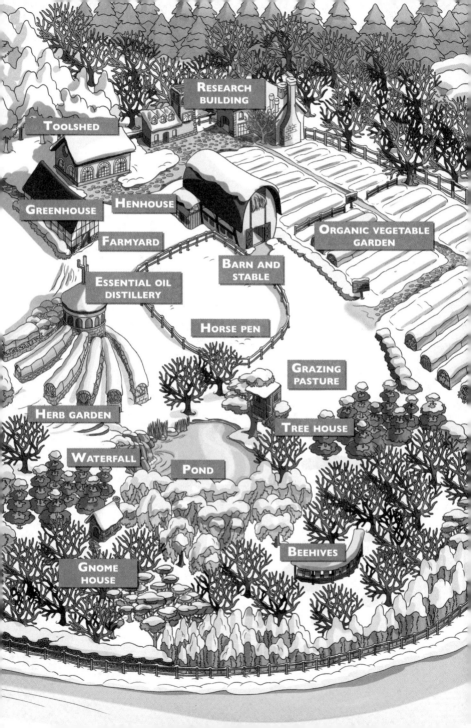

HERE'S THE INSIDE OF THE FARMHOUSE!

1. Entrance
2. Stairs
3. Pantry
4. Library
5. Bathroom
6. Laundry room
7. Kitchen
8. Pizza oven
9. Fireplace
10. Dining room
11. Living room
12. Main fireplace
13. Sitting room
14. Music room
15. Gym
16. Bathroom
17. Patio
18. Guest room

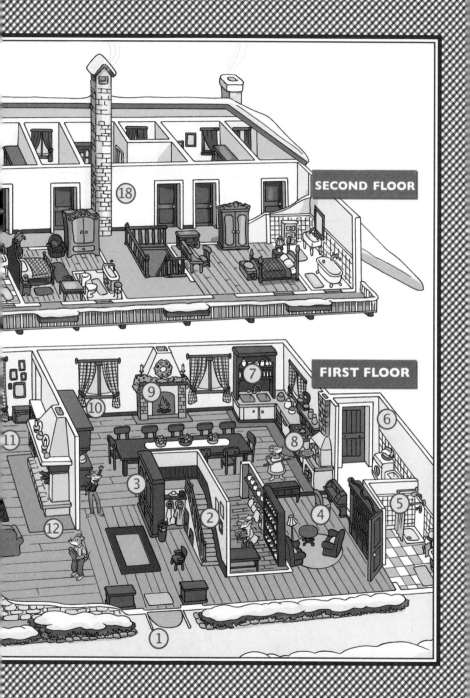

SECOND FLOOR

FIRST FLOOR

I found out so many things I hadn't known about life in the country.

For example, I had to **wake** at dawn every day! Every morning, Tina handed me a very **long** list of daily tasks.

"First, gather **eggs** from the henhouse for breakfast," she squeaked. "Then Farmer Cheddarpaw is coming by to show you how to manage the vegetable garden. After that, collect the **honey** from the beehives and help Yoyo with the **baking**! And don't forget to mow the grass, **milk** the cows, and . . ."

First of all . . .
I'm so tired!

Squeak! There was so much to do and it wasn't even six in the morning. I headed for the henhouse. Alas, the hens weren't happy to see me. OUCH, THE PECKING!

cluck, cluck, cluck!

Bzzz...
Bzzz...

After that, I tried to collect the **honey**, but the bees were too busy **stinging** my tail! When Farmer Cheddarpaw arrived to help me in the vegetable garden, the first thing he did was make me shovel stinky **MANURE**.

"It will really help the crops grow **Faster**," he explained. "Grab a shovel and get some from the barn, Geronimo!"

Finally, I headed back to the kitchen to help Yoyo. She wanted me to pick **blackberries** (the **THORNY** bushes

THE COUNTRYSIDE IS SO BEAUTIFUL!
(Isn't it?)

In the country you don't need an alarm clock: the rooster **wakes** you at dawn.

It's not easy to collect the hens' **eggs**!

When the hens **PECK**, it hurts!

Honey is sweet, but watch out for the bees!

To prepare the vegetable garden, you need **MANURE** . . .

Chestnut butter is delicious, but the BURRS prick!

Ouch!

6

7

Whoops!

When it rains, you can easily SLIP on the wet grass!

8

It's so itchy!

Steer clear of poison ivy!

9

Oops!

Goats like to chew on everything!

10

Help!

Milking cows isn't easy!

were so sharp!), **chestnuts** (the **spiky** burrs prick!), and STINGING NETTLE leaves. OUCH!

Living in the country wasn't always easy cheesy, but we were happy. Every night we sat down together to eat a healthy, delicious meal.

THE SECRET OF THE GREAT OAK

One night I went to bed feeling particularly **exhausted**. I was hoping I could sleep in the next morning, but right at dawn I heard it: cock-a-doodle-doo!

1 It was Hugo, the rooster!

I covered my head and tried to go back to sleep, but something pecked my ear: CLUCK, CLUCK, CLUCK!*

2 It was Lina, the hen!

* *Cluck, cluck, cluck!* means "Wake up, slacker!" in hen.

I pulled the covers over my snout and went back to **sleep**. But a second later someone opened the windows and let in a blast of **COLD AiR** that blew the covers off my bed. Then I heard the clang of a metal fork hitting a gong.

3 **It was Tina Spicytail, the alarm clock!**

"Wake up, sleepyhead!" she squeaked. "Time to get out of bed!"

I got up and looked out the window. The sun wasn't up yet. It was **cold**, but I decided to take a walk. I got bundled up in a jacket, scarf, and hat, and started walking down the **dirt road**. I walked in **silence**, breathing in the cold air, snow crunching under my paws. Finally, I arrived at the **GREAT OAK**!

I wonder how long this tree has been here? I thought to myself. *Who knows how many* **BIRDS** *have made* nests *in its branches? Who knows how many* mice *have taken a cool rest in the* shade of its leaves?

As I studied the tree thoughtfully, I noticed an **OLD STONE** covered in thorns at the foot of the tree. I pushed the thorns aside and began to **read** . . . Great Gouda! I had uncovered a

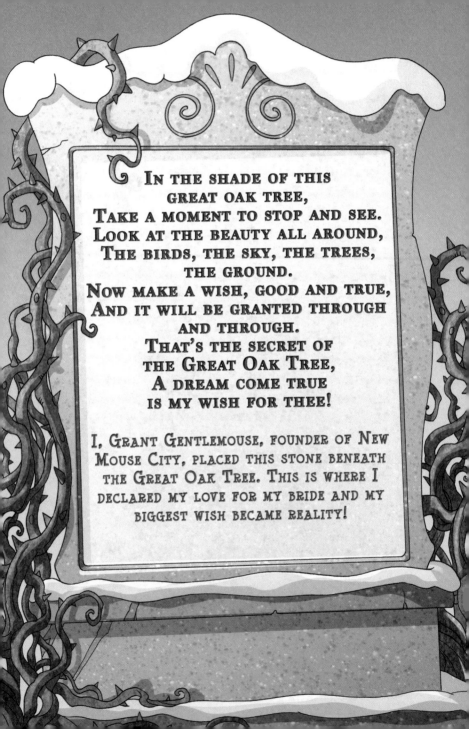

IN THE SHADE OF THIS
GREAT OAK TREE,
TAKE A MOMENT TO STOP AND SEE.
LOOK AT THE BEAUTY ALL AROUND,
THE BIRDS, THE SKY, THE TREES,
THE GROUND.
NOW MAKE A WISH, GOOD AND TRUE,
AND IT WILL BE GRANTED THROUGH
AND THROUGH.
THAT'S THE SECRET OF
THE GREAT OAK TREE,
A DREAM COME TRUE
IS MY WISH FOR THEE!

I, GRANT GENTLEMOUSE, FOUNDER OF NEW
MOUSE CITY, PLACED THIS STONE BENEATH
THE GREAT OAK TREE. THIS IS WHERE I
DECLARED MY LOVE FOR MY BRIDE AND MY
BIGGEST WISH BECAME REALITY!

real *mouserific treasure* at the base of that tree! I couldn't believe that no one else had found the stone in the many years since Grant Gentlemouse had founded **new Mouse City**. I couldn't wait to tell my friends.

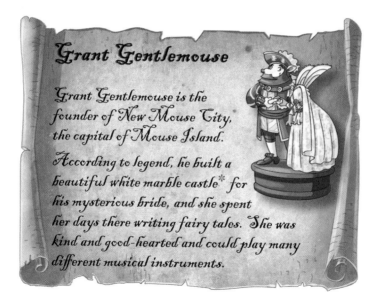

Grant Gentlemouse

Grant Gentlemouse is the founder of New Mouse City, the capital of Mouse Island.

According to legend, he built a beautiful white marble castle* for his mysterious bride, and she spent her days there writing fairy tales. She was kind and good-hearted and could play many different musical instruments.

---

* You can read all about this in my book *The Hunt for the Hundredth Key.*

As I hurried back to tell everyone about my fabumouse **discovery**, I saw the *leopard-patterned* limousine with the tinted windows again.

It had been **months** since I'D LAST SEEN it. What was that STRANGE car doing way out here in the country? It looked much too **fancy** to be zipping around on dirt roads.

Madame No is the CEO of EGO Corp (Enormously Gigantic Organization), a powerful company that handles a lot of real-estate deals on Mouse Island. EGO Corp builds malls and skyscrapers and owns airlines, newspapers, and TV stations. Whenever you ask her a question, she will always answer with one word: "NO!"

One of the car windows was down, and I got a glimpse of an **arrogant-looking** rodent with short fur. She glared at me with eyes as cold as ICE. She was the same rodent I had seen outside the real-estate office, but this time I recognized her: she was none other than the CEO of EGO Corp, **Madame No**!

Holey cheese, what was **she** doing here?!

How strange!

A MYSTERIOUS
MESSAGE . . .

When I walked into the house, my friends
and family were all sitting around the
LARGE KITCHEN TABLE.

The fire **crackled** pleasantly.

"Geronimo, come join us for breakfast!" Creepella squeaked.

"Yes, Tina just baked an **apple pie**!" Thea added.

I sat down at the table with my friends and enjoyed the **freshly baked** warm

BREAKFAST IS THE FIRST MEAL OF THE DAY, SO IT'S IMPORTANT NOT TO SKIP IT!

For a healthy and nutritious breakfast, start with a glass of milk (or a small cup of yogurt).

Follow that with one of these:
- a bowl of cereal
- toast with honey or jam
- a whole-wheat bagel
- a slice of a simple fruit pie

IF YOU NEED TO WAKE UP A LITTLE EARLIER TO MAKE TIME FOR BREAKFAST, DO IT! AND DON'T FORGET TO HAVE A MIDMORNING SNACK LIKE A PIECE OF FRESH FRUIT OR A SLICE OF MULTIGRAIN BREAD WITH NUT BUTTER.

bread, the honey from our beehives, the homemade blueberry jam, and the yogurt and cheese from the milk of our cows.

Yum, yum, yummy!

I told everyone about the stone I had uncovered at the foot of the GREAT OAK TREE, and my friends were all excited about it.

Then we got up from the table and started our activities for the day. A few mice began to read, someone sat down to play the piano, and Benjamin and Trappy began playing a memory card game.

Right then my cell phone beeped: I had a text. As

You already snatched the farm away from me. Now keep your paws off the Great Oak Tree!

soon as I read it, my whiskers began to tremble.

Who would have sent such a **NASTY** text without signing it? And why would anyone want to keep me away from the Great Oak Tree?

I showed my friends the mysterious message right away.

"**How strange!**" they cried.

"This is a very odd text," Thea said thoughtfully. "Someone wants you to stay away from the Great Oak Tree . . . but why?"

Benjamin took out his tablet and did a little research.

"Wow!" he squeaked. "The Great Oak is mentioned in today's news!"

Everyone gathered around Benjamin to read the story.

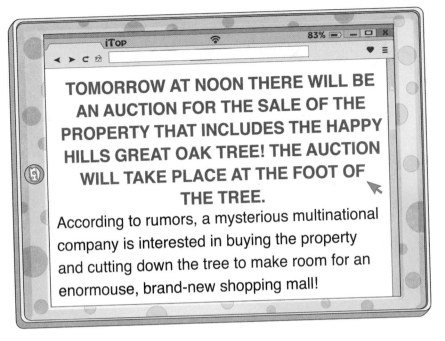

TOMORROW AT NOON THERE WILL BE AN AUCTION FOR THE SALE OF THE PROPERTY THAT INCLUDES THE HAPPY HILLS GREAT OAK TREE! THE AUCTION WILL TAKE PLACE AT THE FOOT OF THE TREE.

According to rumors, a mysterious multinational company is interested in buying the property and cutting down the tree to make room for an enormouse, brand-new shopping mall!

"Really?"

"What's it say?"

"Go ahead and read it!" Tina Spicytail said **encouragingly**.

I shook my snout **SADLY**.

"My dear friends, the **GREAT OAK TREE** is in danger," I said, sighing. "What should we do?"

Everyone replied in unison:

"We will protect the Great Oak!"

TO CATCH A CROOK

Hercule jumped up from the breakfast table and waved a BANANA in the air angrily.

"I'd just love to know who these **cowardly crooks** are who are trying to scare you away, Geronimo!" he cried. "I'm **on the case**, or my name isn't Hercule Poirat! I'll catch them, just wait! We won't be scared away so **easily**, that's for sure!"

"Yeah!" some of the others chimed in.

"Don't be afraid, Geronimo," my friends squeaked. "You're not alone!"

"There's one

If I catch those crooks . . .

other thing you should all know," I said. "This morning when I was walking back from the Great Oak Tree, I saw a long, *leopard-patterned* limousine with **tinted windows**. It was the same car I saw outside the real-estate office when I bought the farm all those months ago. And do you want to know who I saw inside that car?"

"**Of course!**" everyone squeaked.

"Who was it?"

"Come on, Geronimo, *tell us*!"

I took a deep breath. "It was Madame No."

"Holey cheese!" Hercule replied. "That means that EGO Corp must be the one that wants to take down the tree to build a Shopping Mall!"

"What can we do?" I asked.

We tried and tried to come up with a **plan** to protect the Great Oak, but we couldn't think of anything!

Thea, Creepella, and Flora were **whispering** together in a corner. All of a sudden, they became quiet, and Flora turned to the rest of us.

"We have an **idea**!" she squeaked. "There is only one thing we can do to **save** the Great Oak Tree: go to the auction and **win**!"

"That's a good thought, but we will have to come up with enough money to win," I replied. "How can we possibly defeat the powerful, wealthy EGO Corp? And we don't have much time: the auction is tomorrow at noon!"

Benjamin, Trappy, and Bugsy Wugsy whispered to one another. Then they opened

their backpacks and handed me their **piggy banks**.

"Here is everything we have saved, Uncle," Benjamin said. "It's not much, but we want to **help save** the Great Oak, too!"

"Thank you!" I squeaked. "You know, you may be on to something. I'll add my savings, and if all of us contribute just a little bit,

Here are our savings!

Here, Uncle G!

then a small amount will **GR☺W** and **GR☺W** and **GR☺W** until it's a **huge** sum!

"We'll print a special edition of **The Rodent's Gazette** to raise the money to **WIN** the —"

But before I could even finish my sentence, Tina came racing into the room, holding the phone.

Mr. Stilton!

Yikes!

She knocked me right off my paws, and I almost **DROPPED** the piggy banks!

"Mr. Stilton, your grandfather is on the line," she squeaked. "He wants to talk to you RIGHT NOW!"

I put the phone on speaker so everyone could hear my grandfather's voice . . .

WHAT IS AN AUCTION?

An auction is a type of sale in which objects, buildings, or pieces of land are offered for sale to the public. The person who "bids," or offers, the most money wins.

SPECIAL EDITION!

"Grandson!" my grandfather roared. "Tina explained everything to me. For once I agree with you: we absolutely must save the Great Oak! That tree is a special piece of Mouse Island history. It cannot be cut down! We will run a special edition of *The Rodent's Gazette* and all proceeds will go toward the auction. But we need some IDEAS for the newspaper articles."

We must protect the Great Oak!

"We can write about how great it is

to visit or live in the countryside," Flora suggested. "I can contribute by writing a column about **homegrown** herbal teas."

"And we can include a **GAME**, too," Benjamin said. "It can be a nature memory card game like the one Trappy and I have been playing. That would be a special giveaway . . ."

Let's include a memory game!

"Great idea, Benjamin!" Grandfather agreed. "I'm so **proud** of you! We'll get started here at the paper, and we'll put together a fabumouse special issue. The paper will be at newsstands tomorrow morning before **sunrise**! Over and out!"

Then he **hung up**.

My dear readers, the following morning rodents all across Mouse Island snapped up their own issues of the special edition. Within one hour, **The Rodent's Gazette** had **sold out**!

It was a mouserific success!

So many mice!

I'd like a copy!

It's almost our turn!

Will we be able to get one?

We have to save the Great Oak!

For sure!

Now we had enough funds to attend the **auction** and perhaps even win! But I had a feeling it wouldn't be easy to **DEFEAT** Madame No and the EGO Corp.

And my feeling was completely **correct** . . .

ONE POWERFUL MOUSE

I was getting ready to leave for the auction when I heard the **squeal** of car tires and the screeched sound of the brakes.

SCREECH!

Moments later, the doorbell rang loudly:

DING DONG! DING DONG!
DING DONG!

I ran to open the door and saw three **buff**, enormouse rats in *leopard-print* jackets standing there!

"We told you to stay away from the Great Oak, you **smarty-mouse**!"

the first rat growled **MEANLY**.

"Yeah," agreed the second. "Madame No wants to buy that tree, and what Madame No wants, Madame No gets!"

"Be careful," the third rat squeaked, "or you'll make her very, very **angry**!"

My whiskers trembled with fear: what bullies!

Stay away!

Yeah!

Watch out!

Squeak!

But I wasn't going to let them *intimidate* me.

"My friends and I are not afraid," I replied. "Tell Madame No we'll see her at the auction, and we're going to **WIN**!"

The back window of the limousine lowered, and I saw Madame No staring at me with **EYES** as cold as an ICY winter night.

"You'd better watch out!" she hissed. "I'll take down the Great Oak Tree and build a mega shopping mall in its place! I'm one powerful mouse, and you don't want to cross me. I always win, no matter what!"

Then the car screeched off.

At noon we all met at the tree . . .

The auction was about to start!

My heart was beating **quickly**, but I wasn't scared because I knew I wasn't alone!

In fact, many mice I knew (and even some I didn't know!) had come from New Mouse City to support me. It was nice to know so many people cared.

The **auctioneer** announced the beginning of the auction: "Lady rodents and gentlemice, we are here for the sale of the Happy Hills property, which includes the GREAT OAK TREE. The opening bid will be the low price of —"

He cleared his throat and said a number. It was a **huge** amount!

"**Ooohhhh!**" the audience cried out in surprise. Not many mice had that kind of **money**.

"Any bidders?" the auctioneer asked.

Madame No raised her paw.

"I bid **tWiCe** that amount!" she said triumphantly.

I raised my **paw** to bid as well.

"And I offer **tWiCe** that amount!" I squeaked.

Madame No raised her left eyebrow in **surprise**.

"Well . . ." she replied, "I offer **double** the doubled **double** amount!"

Any bidders?

THE AUCTIONEER
During an auction, the auctioneer is the person who announces, describes, and awards items to the highest bidder.

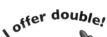

I offer double!

I'll double the doubled amount!

I'll double the doubled double!

I'll bid double the double the doubled double!

I was able to counter her offer thanks to the proceeds from the sale of the special edition of *The Rodent's Gazette*.

"I'll counter that offer with double the double the doubled double!" I squeaked.

Madame No lifted her RIGHT eyebrow (she was completely stunned).

"I'll double the double the double the doubled double!" she shouted.

I stared **straight** at her and proudly replied: "Then I'll bid double the double the double the double the doubled double amount!"

"How dare you!" Madame No

squeaked. I could tell I was really getting under her **FUR**.

"Everyone please pay close attention: I offer double the double the double the double the double the double the doubled double amount! Is that clear?"

I'll double the double the double the double the doubled double!

I placed my final offer, my whiskers trembling from **exhaustion**. I had finally **used up** all the funds raised by the special edition of *The Rodent's Gazette*!

How dare you?

"What are we going to do now, Stilton?" Hercule asked. "There isn't one penny left to offer . . ."

Err . . .

Unfortunately, Madame No's henchmice overheard us squeaking. They immediately advised Madame No.

When Madame No realized I didn't have one penny left, she smirked confidently.

"I offer one penny more than Geronimo Stilton's last bid! What do you have to say now, huh?"

She crossed her paws across her chest and glared at me smugly, confident that she had won.

"Ooohhhh!" the audience gasped. "What will Geronimo Stilton do now?"

"Lady rodents and gentlemice, any other bids?" the auctioneer asked.

I turned as white as mozzarella. That was it: there was no more money I could OFFER. I was going to lose.

I won! I won! I won!

Meanwhile, positive she had won, **Madame No** began to brag.

"You don't have any more money, huh?" she taunted. "Ha! **You lost!** I told you to watch out, rat! You should have known better! I'm **one powerful mouse**, and **I WON, I WON, I WON**! Now I'll tear down that ugly old tree and everyone will finally understand that I'm the boss of Mouse Island! **Me! Madame No!**"

But at that moment, Benjamin pulled the sleeve of my jacket.

"Uncle, it's not over yet!" he squeaked.

He handed me **two coins**.

"I found them at the bottom of my backpack," he squeaked. "They must have

Here, Uncle G!

Thank you!

come out of my **piggy bank**!"

I grabbed the coins, turned toward the auctioneer, and asked **ANXIOUSLY**: "Is it too late? I would like to bid two more pennies! One more penny than Madame No's offer!"

I'm the boss!

The auctioneer nodded. Then he turned to **Madame No**. But she was **shrieking** and **celebrating** so loudly, she hadn't heard my **offer**! And she couldn't hear the auctioneer, either. He asked one more time if there were any last bids.

"**One**...**two**...**three**...

Sold!

Sold to Geronimo Stilton!" the auctioneer cried.

Wait, stop!

"STILTON JUST WON!" the audience shouted **happily**.

"Yay! Hooray for Geronimo Stilton. Hooray for the GREAT OAK TREE!"

Suddenly, Madame No realized that she had missed something.

"Wait, stop!" she squeaked. "What's going on?! We have to do it again!"

"I'm sorry, Madame No," the auctioneer replied, shaking his snout. "Mr. Stilton won the auction, fair and SQUARE."

Yes, I had WON, and we had saved the Great Oak Tree!

We have to do it again!

Sorry, Madame No!

My Wish Is . . .

Since then, every year on **December 21**, the entire Stilton family hosts a **fabumouse party** right at the foot of the Great Oak Tree.

EVERYONE IS WELCOME!

We celebrate how we managed to join forces to **save** the Great Oak. We did it together, just like one big *family*!

And every year, in memory of Grant Gentlemouse and his bride, we hang pieces of paper from the branches of the oak tree. A **wish** is written on each piece of paper.

Would you like to know mine? Each year, it's the same — that we can all live together in **PEACE** and harmony, with respect for one another and for nature! It's a truly *mouserific* wish, isn't it? Together, we can make it come true, or my name isn't **Stilton**, *Geronimo Stilton*!

Good-bye until next time, my dear readers!

Be sure to read all my fabumouse adventures!

#1 Lost Treasure of the Emerald Eye

#2 The Curse of the Cheese Pyramid

#3 Cat and Mouse in a Haunted House

#4 I'm Too Fond of My Fur!

#5 Four Mice Deep in the Jungle

#6 Paws Off, Cheddarface!

#7 Red Pizzas for a Blue Count

#8 Attack of the Bandit Cats

#9 A Fabumouse Vacation for Geronimo

#10 All Because of a Cup of Coffee

#11 It's Halloween, You 'Fraidy Mouse!

#12 Merry Christmas, Geronimo!

#13 The Phantom of the Subway

#14 The Temple of the Ruby of Fire

#15 The Mona Mousa Code

#16 A Cheese-Colored Camper

#17 Watch Your Whiskers, Stilton!

#18 Shipwreck on the Pirate Islands

#19 My Name Is Stilton, Geronimo Stilton

#20 Surf's Up, Geronimo!

#21 The Wild, Wild West

#22 The Secret of Cacklefur Castle

A Christmas Tale

#23 Valentine's Day
Disaster

#24 Field Trip to
Niagara Falls

#25 The Search for
Sunken Treasure

#26 The Mummy
with No Name

#27 The Christmas
Toy Factory

#28 Wedding
Crasher

#29 Down and Out
Down Under

#30 The Mouse Island
Marathon

#31 The Mysterious
Cheese Thief

Christmas Catastrophe

#32 Valley of the
Giant Skeletons

#33 Geronimo and the
Gold Medal Mystery

#34 Geronimo Stilton,
Secret Agent

#35 A Very Merry
Christmas

#36 Geronimo's
Valentine

#37 The Race Across
America

#38 A Fabumouse
School Adventure

#39 Singing Sensation

#40 The Karate Mouse

#41 Mighty Mount
Kilimanjaro

#42 The Peculiar
Pumpkin Thief

#43 I'm Not a
Supermouse!

#44 The Giant
Diamond Robbery

#45 Save the White
Whale!

#46 The Haunted
Castle

#47 Run for the Hills, Geronimo!

#48 The Mystery in Venice

#49 The Way of the Samurai

#50 This Hotel Is Haunted!

#51 The Enormouse Pearl Heist

#52 Mouse in Space!

#53 Rumble in the Jungle

#54 Get into Gear, Stilton!

#55 The Golden Statue Plot

#56 Flight of the Red Bandit

#57 The Stinky Cheese Vacation

#58 The Super Chef Contest

#59 Welcome to Moldy Manor

#60 The Treasure of Easter Island

#61 Mouse House Hunter

#62 Mouse Overboard!

#63 The Cheese Experiment

#64 Magical Mission

#65 Bollywood Burglary

#66 Operation: Secret Recipe

#67 The Chocolate Chase

#68 Cyber-Thief Showdown

#69 Hug a Tree, Geronimo

#70 The Phantom Bandit

Up Next!

Don't miss any of these exciting Thea Sisters adventures!

Thea Stilton and the
Dragon's Code

Thea Stilton and the
Mountain of Fire

Thea Stilton and the
Ghost of the Shipwreck

Thea Stilton and the
Secret City

Thea Stilton and the
Mystery in Paris

Thea Stilton and the
Cherry Blossom Adventure

Thea Stilton and the
Star Castaways

Thea Stilton: Big Trouble
in the Big Apple

Thea Stilton and the
Ice Treasure

Thea Stilton and the
Secret of the Old Castle

Thea Stilton and the
Blue Scarab Hunt

Thea Stilton and the
Prince's Emerald

Thea Stilton and the
Mystery on the Orient Express

Thea Stilton and the
Dancing Shadows

Thea Stilton and the
Legend of the Fire Flowers

Thea Stilton and the
Spanish Dance Mission

Thea Stilton and the
Journey to the Lion's Den

Thea Stilton and the
Great Tulip Heist

Thea Stilton and the
Chocolate Sabotage

Thea Stilton and the
Missing Myth

Thea Stilton and the Lost Letters

Thea Stilton and the Tropical Treasure

Thea Stilton and the Hollywood Hoax

Thea Stilton and the Madagascar Madness

Thea Stilton and the Frozen Fiasco

Thea Stilton and the Venice Masquerade

Thea Stilton and the Niagara Splash

Thea Stilton and the Riddle of the Ruins

And check out my fabumouse special editions!

THEA STILTON: THE JOURNEY TO ATLANTIS

THEA STILTON: THE SECRET OF THE FAIRIES

THEA STILTON: THE SECRET OF THE SNOW

THEA STILTON: THE CLOUD CASTLE

THEA STILTON: THE TREASURE OF THE SEA

THEA STILTON: THE LAND OF FLOWERS

THEA STILTON: THE SECRET OF THE CRYSTAL FAIRIES

Don't miss any of my special edition adventures!

THE KINGDOM OF FANTASY

THE QUEST FOR PARADISE:
THE RETURN TO THE KINGDOM OF FANTASY

THE AMAZING VOYAGE:
THE THIRD ADVENTURE IN THE KINGDOM OF FANTASY

THE DRAGON PROPHECY:
THE FOURTH ADVENTURE IN THE KINGDOM OF FANTASY

THE VOLCANO OF FIRE:
THE FIFTH ADVENTURE IN THE KINGDOM OF FANTASY

THE SEARCH FOR TREASURE:
THE SIXTH ADVENTURE IN THE KINGDOM OF FANTASY

THE ENCHANTED CHARMS:
THE SEVENTH ADVENTURE IN THE KINGDOM OF FANTASY

THE PHOENIX OF DESTINY:
AN EPIC KINGDOM OF FANTASY ADVENTURE

THE HOUR OF MAGIC:
THE EIGHTH ADVENTURE IN THE KINGDOM OF FANTASY

THE WIZARD'S WAND:
THE NINTH ADVENTURE IN THE KINGDOM OF FANTASY

THE SHIP OF SECRETS:
THE TENTH ADVENTURE IN THE KINGDOM OF FANTASY

THE DRAGON OF FORTUNE:
AN EPIC KINGDOM OF FANTASY ADVENTURE

THE JOURNEY THROUGH TIME

BACK IN TIME:
THE SECOND JOURNEY THROUGH TIME

THE RACE AGAINST TIME:
THE THIRD JOURNEY THROUGH TIME

LOST IN TIME:
THE FOURTH JOURNEY THROUGH TIME

NO TIME TO LOSE:
THE FIFTH JOURNEY THROUGH TIME

ABOUT THE AUTHOR

Born in New Mouse City, Mouse Island, **GERONIMO STILTON** is Rattus Emeritus of Mousomorphic Literature and of Neo-Ratonic Comparative Philosophy. For the past twenty years, he has been running *The Rodent's Gazette*, New Mouse City's most widely read daily newspaper.

Stilton was awarded the Ratitzer Prize for his scoops on *The Curse of the Cheese Pyramid* and *The Search for Sunken Treasure*. He has also received the Andersen 2000 Prize for Personality of the Year. One of his bestsellers won the 2002 eBook Award for world's best ratlings' electronic book. His works have been published all over the globe.

In his spare time, Mr. Stilton collects antique cheese rinds and plays golf. But what he most enjoys is telling stories to his nephew Benjamin.

1. Main entrance
2. Printing presses (where the books and newspaper are printed)
3. Accounts department
4. Editorial room (where the editors, illustrators, and designers work)
5. Geronimo Stilton's office
6. Helicopter landing pad

THE RODENT'S
GAZETTE

Brigand's Isle

This way to the Rodent Straits

Tomcat Island

Pirate Ship of Cats

2

3

4

1

6

7

Cat's Claw Bay

Panther Archipelago

Hamster Islands

Blue Dolphin Bay

5

Swissville

Coral Reefs

25

8

This way to the Mousific Ocean

9

14

Stray Cat Harbor

11

13

12

Cheddarton

10

23

Mouseport

32

15

21

This way to the Ratlantic Ocean

San Mouscisco

22

20

29

19

26

17

16

New Mouse City

18

35

24

30

Mousefort Beach

28

27

31

36

33

37

34

Furflung Island

N

W   E

S

MOUSE ISLAND

This way to the Sea of Mice

Map of Mouse Island

Dear mouse friends,
Thanks for reading, and farewell
till the next book.
It'll be another whisker-licking-good
adventure, and that's a promise!

Geronimo Stilton